Disney PRINCESS
Christmas Adventures

PRINCESS1041

Code is valid for your Disney Princess ebook
and may be redeemed through the Disney
Story Central app on the App Store.
Content subject to availability.
Parent permission required.
Code expires on December 31, 2019.

Parragon

Bath • New York • Cologne • Melbourne • Delhi
Hong Kong • Shenzhen • Singapore

One winter's day, Cinderella
tells the prince she would like
to host a Christmas party at
the castle. The prince agrees
it's a wonderful idea.

Cinderella starts to make the castle look festive. Her friends, Gus and Jaq, help decorate the stairs with a pretty red ribbon.

Help Cinderella by adding pretty bows to the staircase.

Next, Cinderella and the mice decorate the hallways of the castle with pretty garlands. Cinderella uses a ladder to reach the high arches above the doors.

Can you add the stockings to the picture?

Finally, Cinderella hangs some stockings by the warm fireplace, ready for Santa to fill with gifts.

Cinderella insists on doing all the party preparation herself. The housekeeper is surprised—a princess doesn't usually do these kinds of chores.

Use your stickers to complete the scene.

Once everything is laid out, Cinderella feels it doesn't look quite right.
Just then, the Fairy Godmother appears! With a wave of her magic wand, she adds a beautiful swan-shaped ice statue to the table. Cinderella is delighted!

The Fairy Godmother doesn't want to hurt Cinderella's feelings, but the party table needs a little more work. . . .

Once Cinderella has left the room, the Fairy Godmother waves her wand again and creates a wonderful Christmas banquet!

Help create the banquet with your stickers.

Now that everything is ready, the housekeeper asks Cinderella when the guests will be arriving. The princess announces that no other guests are coming—the party is just for the castle staff and their animal friends. Everybody is thrilled.

The castle pets enjoy some delicious festive food. Cinderella gives them gifts that she made herself. Everyone is having a lovely time.

Complete the scene with your stickers!

The castle workers are enjoying the party, too. They feel wonderful to be dancing alongside Cinderella and the prince.

The prince tells Cinderella that she is the kindest person he knows. Cinderella is happy that everybody enjoyed a wonderful Christmas treat.

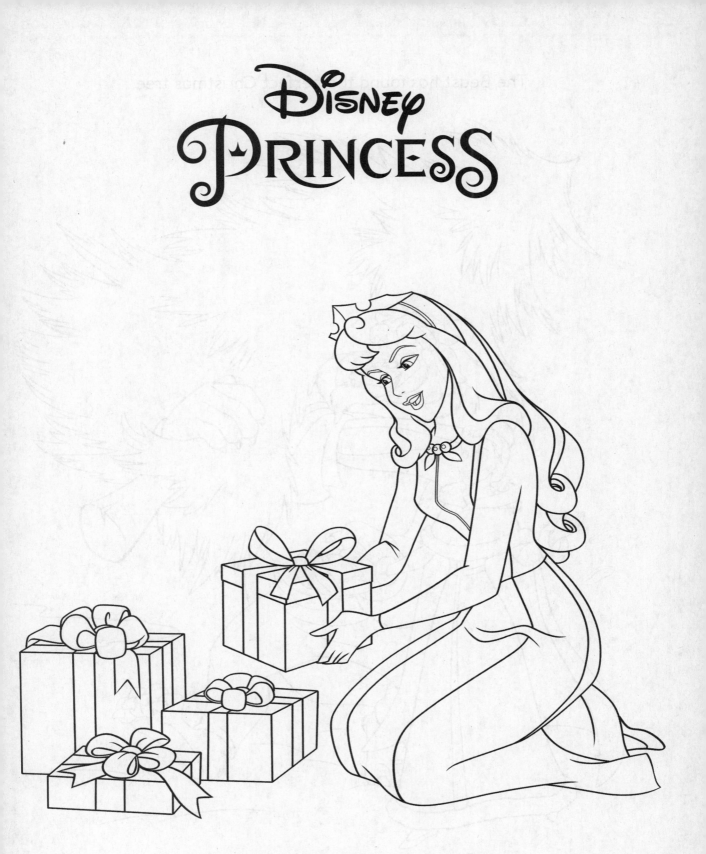

The Beast has found the perfect Christmas tree.

Belle wants the tree to look beautiful for the Christmas ball.

Lumiere admires the lovely tree.

Draw lines to connect the matching Christmas decorations.

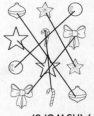

The Beast loves holiday treats!

Christmas is the best time of year.

Sebastian is helping Ariel with her Christmas wrapping.

Ariel and Eric enjoy a delicious feast on Christmas Day.

Sebastian enjoys some Christmas treats, too!

Eric loves his gift from Ariel.

Princess Aurora loves preparing for Christmas.

She asks the Good Fairies to help her decorate the castle.

The fairies make the castle look very festive.

Aurora's little animal friends are helping, too.

Aurora hangs stockings on the fireplace.

Decorate your own Christmas stocking!

Princess Aurora and Prince Phillip meet under the mistletoe.

What a wonderful Christmas!

The royal couple is throwing a Christmas party.

Jasmine and Aladdin share a Christmas dance.
The bottom picture is mixed up. Can you label
the strips in the correct order, from one to five?

1   2   3   4   5

33

Cinderella has been given so many gifts!
How many can you count?

There are _____ gifts.

Answer: There are 11 gifts.

Little Gus gives Cinderella a Christmas kiss!

Help Snow White finish her snowman.
Draw on a face and some buttons.

The Dwarfs want to play!

Snow White and Dopey love to make snow angels.

Everybody warms up in front of the fire.

Snow White bakes Christmas cookies for her friends.

Snow White and the Dwarfs have baked some yummy Christmas cookies. Can you write the letter of the cookie that comes next in each row?

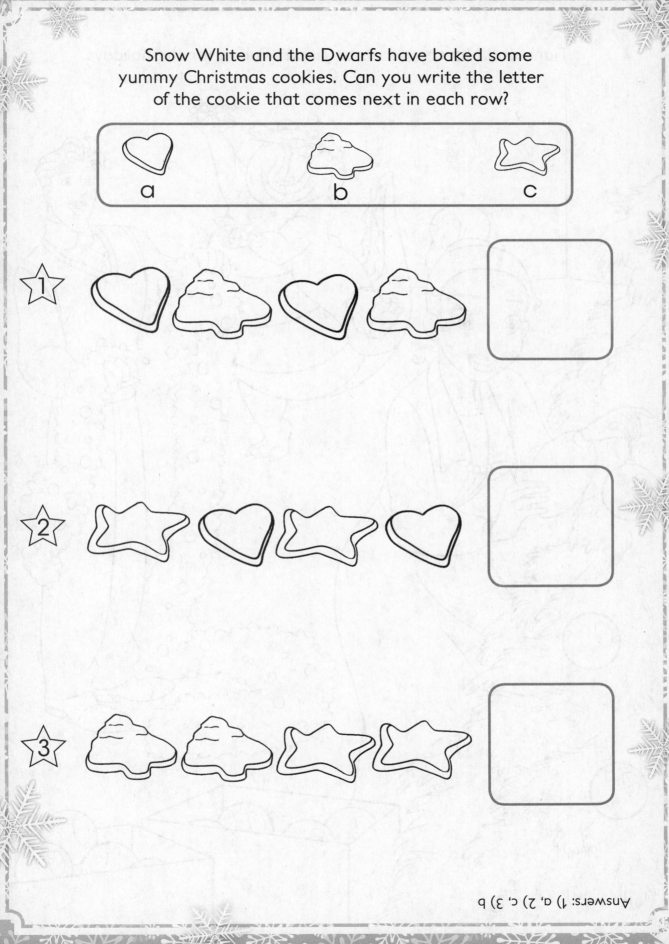

Tiana and Naveen decorate Tiana's Palace for the holidays.

The Christmas tree looks beautiful!

Tiana and Naveen are happy to be spending Christmas together.